When I Grow Bigger

For Kieron, Natalie, Leanne, and Sam
"Oh, to see everything through your eyes,
surprise after surprise after SURPRISE!"
T.C.

For little Camelia and Angelica
and Tiziana
J.B.-B.

Text copyright © 1994 by Trish Cooke
Illustrations copyright © 1994 by John Bendall-Brunello

All rights reserved.

First U.S. edition 1994
Published in Great Britain in 1994 by Walker Books Ltd., London.

Library of Congress Cataloging-in-Publication Data

Cooke, Trish.
When I grow bigger / written by Trish Cooke ; illustrated by John Bendall-Brunello.—1st U.S. ed.
Summary: Baby Thomas is jealous of the bigger kids until, with his father's help,
he becomes bigger than everyone.
ISBN 1-56402-430-X (reinforced trade ed.)
[1. Size—Fiction.]   I. Bendall-Brunello, John, ill.   II. Title.
PZ7.C77494Wh   1994   [E]—dc20   93-42601

2 4 6 8 10 9 7 5 3 1

Printed in Italy

The pictures in this book were done in watercolor and pencil.

Candlewick Press
2067 Massachusetts Avenue
Cambridge, Massachusetts 02140

When I Grow Bigger

TRISH COOKE

illustrated by

JOHN BENDALL-BRUNELLO

CANDLEWICK PRESS
CAMBRIDGE, MASSACHUSETTS

"When I grow bigger,
I'm going to reach
up, up, up
to the ceiling,"
said Leanne.

"When I grow bigger,
I'm going to reach
up, up, up
to the clouds,"
said Sam.

"When I grow bigger,
I'm going to reach
up, up, up
to the sky,"
said Natalie.

Thomas looked
up at them.
They were like three
tall towers . . .

and they looked
down at him
and laughed . . .

"You're just a baby," said Natalie, patting Thomas on the head.

"You're just a nipper," said Sam, bending down to look at Thomas.

But Thomas wriggled and squirmed until he got free.
Leave me alone, Thomas thought.
But the words didn't come out, just YAAGHs and YELLs.

"You're just a little 'un," said Leanne, trying to pick Thomas up.

And that's what they did—
they left Thomas alone,
all alone sitting by
Thomas's dad's daffodils.

And THEY,
the three BIG people,
went off to play in
Thomas's dad's
wheelbarrow.

"You get in,"
said Natalie.

"I want to push,"
said Natalie.

"Let me,"
said Sam.

Thomas watched THEM,
the three BIG people,
playing.

"I'll push," said Sam.

"You can't, you're too small!" said Leanne.

"Get off," said Leanne.

And she grabbed the handles of Thomas's dad's wheelbarrow.

Thomas watched
THEM,
the three BIG people.

"Ow!" said Natalie.
"You!" said Sam.

"I'm telling!"
said Leanne,
running toward
the house.

Along came Thomas's dad's feet.
Thomas didn't look up but
he knew they were Dad's feet
because he had green boots on.
(Mom's are red!)
Dad's green boots
stopped by the daffodils.
He nearly tripped
over Thomas.

"Oooops! Didn't
see you there!"
said Dad.

Thomas was not happy.
Then Dad stooped down
to pick Thomas up.
But Thomas wriggled
and squirmed
and tried
to get free.

"Hey, what's up?"
Dad asked Leanne.

And Leanne yelled,
"THEY'RE FIGHTING!"

So Thomas's dad
held on tight
to Thomas
and ran.

"He started it," said Natalie.

"No, I didn't," said Sam.

Leanne caught up and huffed and puffed.

"Okay, okay," said Thomas's dad. "I don't want to know—just play properly, all of you! I'll be watching!"

Thomas's dad put Thomas in the wheelbarrow. Natalie and Sam took the handles and Leanne looked mad.

"What should we do now?" Leanne said.

"Let's give Thomas a ride!" said Natalie.

And Sam sat down.

Thomas looked
over the side of
the wheelbarrow.
It was a long
way down.

"The baby wants to get out," said Natalie.

"Okay, okay," said Sam.

"I'll do it," said Leanne.

Thomas's dad looked over, so Natalie helped Leanne get Thomas out. Sam held the handles of Thomas's dad's wheelbarrow.

"No, I will," said Natalie.

"You'd be a lot more fun if you were bigger," said Leanne.

"Yes, I wish you'd hurry up and grow big!" said Sam.

Natalie shook her head. "Ah, he's just a baby," she said.

"Humph." Leanne moaned.

"What should we do now?" Sam yawned.

"I don't know," said Natalie.

"I know," said Leanne.

And she started to go toward the house. Thomas's dad was watching, so Natalie and Sam held Thomas's hand.

"Come on,"
said Sam.

"Hurry up,"
whispered Leanne.

Natalie sighed.
"What are we
doing now?"

"We're going to
do something,"
said Leanne.

"What?"
asked Sam.

"Yes, what?"
said Natalie.

"MAKE
THOMAS
GROW!"
Leanne
said.

"YAAAGH!"

cried Thomas.

Dad stopped and smiled.
"What are you up to?"
Thomas's dad said.

"Nothing,"
said Natalie,

"Nothing,"
said Sam,

"Nothing,"
said Leanne,

and they
went inside.

"I'll hold his hands,"
said Leanne.

"I'll hold his feet,"
said Sam.

"What about me?"
said Natalie.

"What about you?"
said Thomas's dad.

"We're only playing,"
said Natalie
and Sam
and Leanne.

Thomas put his
arms up to Dad.

Dad picked him up. Thomas was almost as high as the ceiling!

And then Thomas's dad went outside. Thomas was almost as high as the clouds.

Thomas's hands were up in the air, almost as high as the sky. And Thomas was laughing!

Natalie and Sam and
Leanne watched.

"When I grow bigger . . ."
said Leanne,

"Oh, be quiet,"
said Sam,

"Yes, be quiet,"
said Natalie.

And they all were
looking up, up, up
at BIG Thomas
having fun!

E
COO   Cooke, Trish

           When I grow big-
           ger

DUE DATE	BRODART	07/95	13.95
MAY 2 3	APR 9		
	OCT 2 6 N3		
	NOV 3 N3		
OCT 8	DEC 1 4		
OCT 1 6			
Oct 17			
OCT 2 3			
OCT 3 1			
NOV 8			
NOV 2 1			
NOV 2 7			